THE WONDERFUL WORLD OF WORDS

The Queen Takes Action

Dr Lubna Alsagoff
PhD (Stanford)

 **Marshall Cavendish**
Children

Queen Veronica Vanderbilt Verb made sure that everything ran smoothly in the kingdom of WOW.

Carpenters could build homes for the people of WOW.

Teachers could teach their students.

Regular verbs follow rules.
Present tense verb + ed -> past tense

paint → painted   spray → sprayed
help → helped   train → trained
need → needed   work → worked

Doctors could examine their patients.

Firemen could rescue animals and people.

When the queen had time, she loved to help the actors at the WOW Theatre.

Instead of just walking across the room, maybe he could...

...stride across the room.

...stomp across the room.

...tiptoe across the room.

...crawl across the room.

The queen often taught the actors different ways of speaking:

If you're angry,
you could scream or yell.

If you're sad,
you could wail or moan.

If you're being quiet,
you could whisper.

If you're angry and loud,
you could bellow
or shout or roar.

The king often laughed at all the funny things that happened at the theatre.

He giggled.

He chuckled.

He chortled.

He cackled.

He guffawed.

The queen, however, was quite serious about what she did. It was important that the people of WOW could use the best verbs to describe their actions.

One day, the king received a letter from a very worried farmer.

The king decided he should set out at once to help the farmer.

He asked the queen to come with him.

And he also invited a plumber and a carpenter to come with them.

They all squeezed into the queen's car and set out for the farm at once.

The king walked over to the farmer's horse.

To his surprise,
Nellie began to hop!

Then, the strangest thing happened!

At the pond, the king and queen found
Reggie the rooster trying to paddle!

And then Reggie uttered the strangest sound!

Moooo!

Out in the field, the king and queen were surprised
to see Katie the cow trying to gallop.

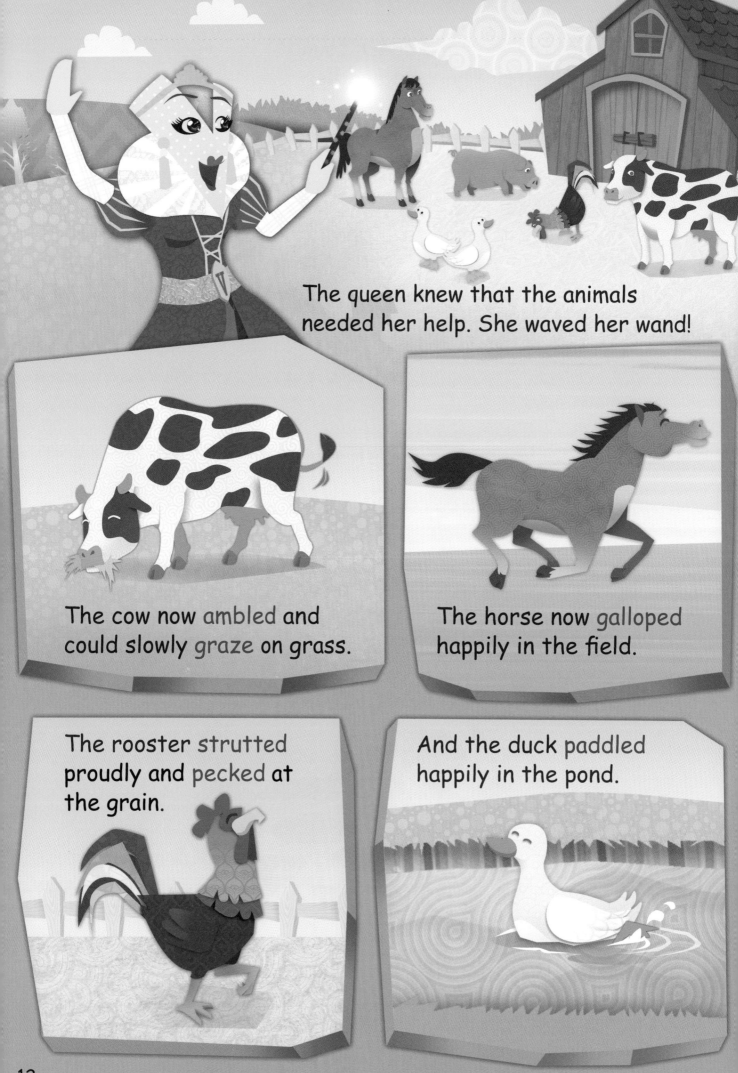

The queen knew that the animals needed her help. She waved her wand!

The cow now ambled and could slowly graze on grass.

The horse now galloped happily in the field.

The rooster strutted proudly and pecked at the grain.

And the duck paddled happily in the pond.

Let's also help the animals make the right sounds!

moo

neigh

quack

meow

bark

crow

oink

cluck

13

The farmer was so happy that the queen could help her animals.

She jumped for joy.

She thanked the queen.

She bowed to the king.

She kissed Katie the cow.

She patted Nellie the horse.

She danced with Danny the duck.

And she tickled Reggie the rooster!

15

The Fabulous Forest of WOW

In the Forest of WOW, Owl, Squirrel, Rabbit and Donkey planned to go on a picnic.

In a basket, Rabbit packed a bunch of bananas, a dozen apples, two big bunches of grapes and five bottles of apple juice.

Rabbit also packed lots of carrots and a big box of chocolate chip cookies.

The animals set off early in the morning. They wanted to have their picnic on a grassy field high up on a hill. It was pretty and had a nice view.

Owl flew ahead.

Donkey trotted happily along the forest path.

Squirrel scampered quickly behind him.

Rabbit was so excited.
He hopped and leapt as fast as he could!

The picnic site was very far away. The animals soon grew tired.

Donkey now trudged slowly.

Rabbit was limping.

Squirrel hobbled painfully up the hill.

Owl could hardly flap his wings.

Finally, they reached the top of the hill.

The minute they laid the blanket on the grass, Donkey opened the picnic basket. Before the other animals could even sit down on the blanket...

...Donkey had gobbled down five sandwiches.

He had munched on the cookies.

He had chomped on the carrots.

He had crunched on so many apples.

He had swallowed half the grapes!

And he had gulped down a whole bottle of apple juice!

When they saw what Donkey was doing...

...Squirrel gasped.

Oh no!

...Owl sighed.

Oh dear!

...Rabbit grumbled.

Leave some food for us, Donkey!

Donkey wailed.

I'm sorry but I was so so hungry!

But thankfully, there was enough food.

And the animals enjoyed their picnic very much!

Find the verbs in the puzzle.

The words can go in any direction. The words can share letters as they cross over each other.

chomp	crunch	enjoy	sign
flap	fly	gasp	trudge
gobble	grumble	gulp	swallow
hobble	hop	leap	wail
limp	munch	scamper	trot

```
V Q N S E L Q Z A O I S G S L
W S C O G O Q M P C W U N I I
Q F C P R U F B A A L U S G A
W E M A U V G J L P A J K H W
E I W X M C B L F G A S P G J
L G G O B P O T Y L M E M G T
H N D C L W E O K D S B O Z I
D C F U E R J R Q G M U N C H
U D N T R N R P D Y O M P L R
X D P U E T B A X S G B M B S
Q Z X W R P Q E V F K O B A S
P M O H C C O L T O R T O L J
X W Y Z B F O H U B P Q D O E
E L B B O H Q I M Y D U N O A
F T R F G L B O C R C V D S Y
```

Use the right verbs to name these actions.

Dear Parents,

In this volume, we look at verbs and how they describe actions. Help your child develop their vocabulary. Instead of using just one verb *walk* or *talk*, children will learn how these actions can be described using a variety of verbs.

Page	Possible Answers

13

horse — neigh
cow — moo
rooster — cluck
duck — quack
chicken — crow
pig — oink
cat — meow
dog — bark

14–15

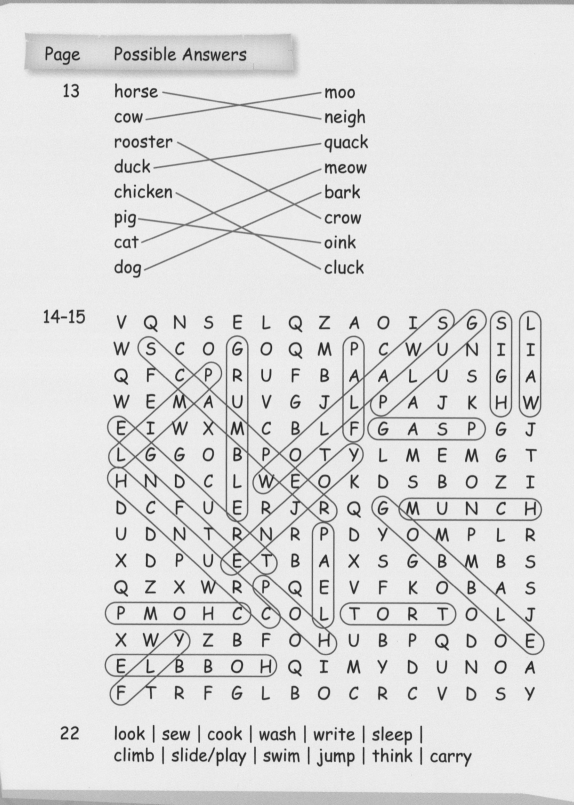

22   look | sew | cook | wash | write | sleep |
climb | slide/play | swim | jump | think | carry

CERTIFICATE OF ACHIEVEMENT

Volume 15

Awarded to

Name _____

for mastering Volume 15

Date _____

Welcome to the **Wonderful World of Words (WOW)**!

This series of books aims to help children learn English grammar in a fun and meaningful way through stories.

Children will read and discover how the people and animals of WOW learn the importance of grammar, as the adventure unfolds from volume to volume.

What's Inside

Imaginative stories that engage children, and help develop an interest in learning grammar

Adventures that encourage children to learn and understand grammar, and not just memorise rules

Games and activities to reinforce learning and check for understanding

About the Author

Dr Lubna Alsagoff is a language educator who is especially known for her work in improving the teaching of grammar in schools and in teacher education. She was Head of English Language and Literature at the National Institute of Education (NIE), and has published a number of grammar resources used by teachers and students. She has a PhD in Linguistics from Stanford University, USA, and has been teaching and researching English grammar for over 30 years.

Published by Marshall Cavendish Children
An imprint of Marshall Cavendish International

A member of the
Times Publishing Group

Printed in Singapore

visit our website at:
www.marshallcavendish.com

Marshall Cavendish
Children

CHILDREN
ISBN 978-981-5009-04-0

9 789815 009040